HEADACHES

HEADACHES

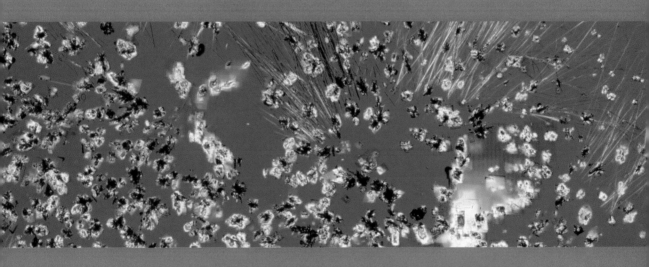

Rick Petreycik

Marshall Cavendish
Benchmark
New York

With thanks to Andrew Hershey, M.D., Ph.D, Associate Professor of Pediatrics and Neurology, University of Cincinnati, and Director, Headaches Center, Children's Hospital Medical Center, Cincinnati, Ohio, for his expert review of the manuscript.

Marshall Cavendish Benchmark
99 White Plains road
Tarrytown, New York 10591-9001
www.marshallcavendish.us

This book is not intended for use as a substitute for advice, consultation, or treatment by a licensed medical practitioner. The reader is advised that no action of a medical nature should be taken without consultation with a licensed medical practitioner, including action that may seem to be indicated by the contents of this work, since individual circumstances vary and medical standards, knowledge, and practices change with time. The publisher, author, and medical consultants disclaim all liability and cannot be held responsible for any problems that may arise from the use of this book.

Library of Congress Cataloging-in-Publication Data

Petreycik, Rick.
  Headaches / by Rick Petreycik.
       p. cm. — (Health alert)
  Summary: "Explores the history, causes, symptoms, treatments, and future of different types of headaches"—Provided by publisher.
  Includes index.
  ISBN-13: 978-0-7614-2210-5
  ISBN-10: 0-7614-2210-2
  1. Headache—Juvenile literature. I. Title. II. Series: Health alert (New York, N.Y.)

  RC392.P45 2007
  616.8'491—dc22

                          2006015815

Front cover: Computer graphic of headache sufferer
Title page: Serotonin
Contents page: X ray of a human skull
Photo research by Candlepants, Inc.
Front cover: Science Photo Library
Cover Photo: Photo Researchers Inc./ Roger Harris/Science Photo Library

The photographs in this book are used by permission and through the courtesy of: *Photo Researchers Inc*: Alfred Pasieka, 3, 12; Erich Schrempp, 5, 17; Jeffrey Greenberg, 10; Charing Cross Hospital, 13; Mike Bluestone, 15; AJ Photo, 18; John Bavosi, 20; Mehua Kulyk, 21; Cordelia Molloy, 22; Mark Clarke, 23; LADA, 25; Neil Borden, 26; Phanie, 27; Jean-Loup Charmet, 34; Omikron, 35; Deep Light Productions, 36; Carolyn A. McKeone, 37, 44; Damien Lovegrove, 38; Will & Deni McIntyre, 40; Mike Agiliolo, 41; David Grossman, 43; Mark Harmel, 46; S. Fraser, 48; Holt Studios, 49; Coneyl Jay, 51; Bettina Solomon, 52; Martin Dohrn, 53; Oscar Burriel, 54. *Illustration Copyright* © *2006 Nucleus Medical Art, All rights reserved*. www.nucleusinc.com: 11. *Art Resource, New York*: Scala, 31; Snark, 32. *Corbis*: Ole Graf/zefa, 45.

Printed in China
6 5 4 3 2 1

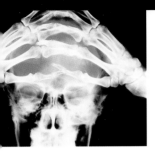

CONTENTS

1

WHAT IS IT LIKE TO HAVE HEADACHES?

JACK'S HEADACHE

When eleven-year-old Jack got home after a quick soccer game with his friends, he was tired, hungry, and thirsty. He stayed up late the night before to work on a report. At school, he skipped lunch to finish the report. Then after school, Jack and his friends got so caught up in their game, they forgot to take water breaks. Now he had a headache that made him feel like a rubber band was squeezing his head. Lying on his bed, Jack told his mother that his head hurt.

She said he was probably **dehydrated** from not drinking enough water on such a hot day. She explained that people could get headaches from skipping meals or forgetting to drink water or a sports drink while playing sports on a hot day. She said she would get him some water, a snack, and a cold cloth for his forehead. She also wanted Jack to rest before dinner.

In a few minutes, Jack's mother returned with a big glass of water and an **ibuprofen** tablet. After he drank all the water, Jack took a few bites of the apple and crackers his mother had left for him. Then he lay back on his bed again with the cold cloth on his forehead. After a while, he removed the cloth and took a nap. By the time dinner rolled around, Jack's headache was completely gone.

CAITLIN'S MIGRAINES

Caitlin's **migraine** headaches were not just aches, but sharp pains. Before the pain actually started, Caitlin sometimes knew when one was coming because she began to feel dizzy and a little sick to her stomach. When the migraine pain did arrive, she felt as if someone were hammering a nail into one spot in her head over and over again. It was awful! After several minutes, the pain would spread to the entire right side of Caitlin's head and then to the opposite side. The pain often grew so bad, Caitlin would lie down in her room with the shades down. Any light and noise made the migraine pain worse. Sometimes she could barely focus her eyes until the headache was gone, and it could take a whole day to go away.

Caitlin remembered her first visit to the **neurologist.** He was a doctor who specialized in headaches and problems with the brain. Caitlin was only ten at the time. She and her parents had visited him to find out what could be done about the migraines. Her father also suffered from migraines, but Caitlin's parents wanted to make sure the headaches their daughter had were not a sign of some other condition.

During that visit, the neurologist asked Caitlin a lot of

questions. He wanted to know how often she had headaches, where she felt the headache pain the most, how painful it was, and how long it usually lasted. He also asked her to describe how she felt right before the pain started. He questioned her about her eating and sleeping habits. He checked her eyes, ears, and throat.

When he had finished his exam, the neurologist told Caitlin and her parents that her headaches were migraines. They were not due to any other medical problems. He said that the tendency to get migraines ran in families, and that Caitlin had probably inherited the tendency from her father.

The doctor gave Caitlin some tips to help prevent the migraines and to manage those she did get. He advised her to get plenty of sleep and to go to bed and wake up at roughly the same time every day. He said it was very important for Caitlin to eat at regular times of the day so she did not get too hungry. Since Caitlin played sports, the doctor told her how important it was to drink fluids before playing and during breaks, especially if it was hot out. He told Caitlin's parents how much ibuprofen to give her as soon as she felt a migraine coming on.

Caitlin had been following the neurologist's advice ever since. On weekends, she tried not to go to bed too late or sleep in for too long. She ate healthy meals at regular times. While participating in sports, she always drank plenty of water and

Many migraine sufferers often have their first migraine headaches as children.

sports drinks to replace important nutrients her body lost when she sweated.

When Caitlin did feel a migraine coming on, she took the ibuprofen. This often kept the headache from getting worse or lasting too long. By the time she was a teenager, Caitlin suffered from fewer migraine headaches. And those she did get did not bother her as much as they had in the past.

2

WHAT IS A HEADACHE?

Headache pain is a sign that tells you some part of your body hurts and needs attention. If you do not get enough food and water for your body to work properly, those conditions can **trigger** a headache. If you get sick, have certain infections, or hit your head too hard, you may also get a headache. Although they are rare, abnormalities in the brain can cause headaches, too.

You might think your brain or skull hurt during a headache, but they do not feel a thing. That is because they lack pain-sensitive

Sometimes the throbbing pains from a headache can seem unbearable. But with proper treatment, headaches can be managed.

nerve cells, which transmit messages throughout the body to and from your brain and spinal column. However, other places near your brain are packed with nerve cells that do cause you to feel headache pain. Many of these nerves are located in the **blood vessels** and muscles in your head and neck. There are also pain-sensitive nerve cells in your scalp and in the **meninges,** a protective covering for the brain. Some special nerves in your face, throat, and mouth also have many pain-sensitive nerve cells.

All these areas are part of your body's major pain pathway called the **trigeminal nerve system.** This system runs from the brain stem at the top of your spine to your face and head. It is made up of sensitive nerve fibers that make it possible for you to feel different physical sensations, including headache pain.

Some experts believe headaches develop when problems somewhere in the body set off nerve activity in the brain. The problems may be an illness like the flu or a condition like ongoing back pain. A person with an inherited tendency to get migraines

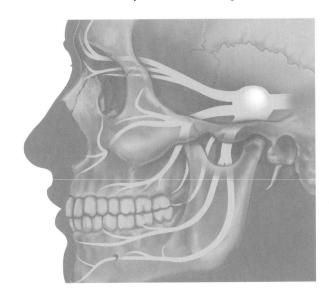

Your head can hurt all over as pain messages travel over the many pain pathways of the trigeminal nerve, which runs through your face, mouth, and jaws.

The neurotransmitter serotonin is a powerful chemical that keeps blood vessels at the best size for blood flow. Changing levels of serotonin can cause headaches.

is especially sensitive to medical conditions and triggers such as irregular sleep patterns, hunger, and thirst. It is believed that nerve activity in the brain may change the body's levels of **neurotransmitters.** These important chemical messengers include **endorphins, serotonin,** and **dopamine.** Migraine sufferers probably have lower levels of some of these important chemicals.

Normally, endorphins help ease pain. Serotonin helps regulate moods, sleep, and blood vessel size. Dopamine helps regulate blood flow. When nerve activity in the brain causes changes in neurotransmitter levels, the result may be a headache. These chemical changes, in turn, irritate blood vessels and pain centers. For migraine sufferers, the process can quickly become very painful. That is because people who get migraines are less able than others to regulate changes or make up for their lower levels of neurotransmitters.

Most other people with an ordinary headache have a greater ability to regulate chemical messengers if they take steps to rest when they are tired, drink water when they are thirsty, and eat when they are hungry. If those steps do not work, the lowest dose of ibuprofen will probably make the headache go away. Migraine sufferers, on the other hand, may need higher doses of ibuprofen or possibly other headache medications. When a headache is a symptom of an illness or an underlying condition, then those conditions must be treated.

Researchers continue to investigate the interaction of the body's **nervous system** with the trigeminal nerve system, blood vessels, and the body's pain centers. Improved imaging

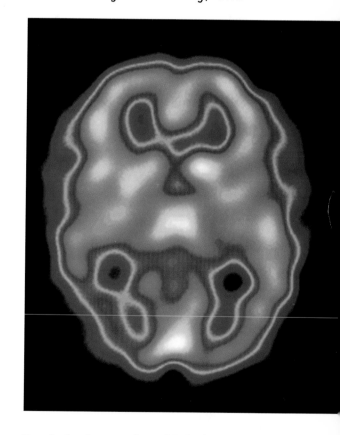

New technology, such as this brain scan, can show a migraine while it is taking place.

machines that allow doctors to measure or to look directly at brain activity will help researchers continue the search for the causes and treatment of headaches.

WHO GETS HEADACHES?

If you want to see how common headaches are, just walk down the aisle of any drugstore and notice the number of headache medications on the shelves. Those do not include the many **prescription** medications that doctors order for patients who get repeated headaches or migraines. Next to toothaches, headaches are the next most-common cause of pain that people suffer. Along with backaches, headaches prompt more doctor visits than any other medical problem. Nearly all adults, teenagers, and children get headaches once in a while. More than 50 million headache sufferers get repeated headaches that cause them to miss school or work. If you added them all up, people who get migraines miss more than 157 million days of school or work every year.

TYPES OF HEADACHES

If you are like most people, you probably have had headaches when you were sick with the flu or other illnesses. Or perhaps you got a headache after you bumped your head too hard or let yourself get too tired or hungry. Eyestrain can cause headaches in people who need glasses or who read too long without a break. Others get headaches after stopping or starting certain medications. You may have experienced an ice-cream headache after eating something very cold too fast. That was due to the nerve cells in the trigeminal nerve system near your throat reacting to the cold.

Headaches come in many varieties, depending on their causes and the kind of pain **symptoms** a person experiences. Many experts group headaches into two categories. **Primary headaches** arrive by themselves and are not due to underlying health problems. However, infections, underlying medical conditions, injuries, and brain abnormalities may cause **secondary headaches.**

Staring at a computer screen for a long time can cause eyestrain that may lead to headaches.

PRIMARY HEADACHES

Nearly 90 percent of headaches are primary headaches. They fall into three groups: **tension-type headaches,** migraines, and **cluster headaches.**

Tension-Type Headaches

Tension-type headaches are the most common and usually cause less severe pain than migraines. They are called tension-type headaches because headache sufferers feel as if their heads, necks, or their temples on the sides of their heads, are being squeezed. Sometimes this squeezing feels like a mild, dull ache all over the head. Other times, the pressure is more painful.

Researchers once believed that tension-type headaches occurred when muscles near the head and spinal cord tightened or blood vessels either expanded or got smaller. However, current research shows that the headache starts first, *then* affects pain-sensitive muscles and blood vessels. Whatever the cause, a person with a tension-type headache usually feels a steady, aching pain on both sides of the head. In children, intense pain on both sides is likely to be a migraine.

Many kinds of triggers can set off tension-type headaches. You may have had a tension-type headache after skipping a meal or oversleeping. Since your body needs regular sleep, food, and water to work properly, a tension-type headache can signal that you need to get some rest or something to eat or drink.

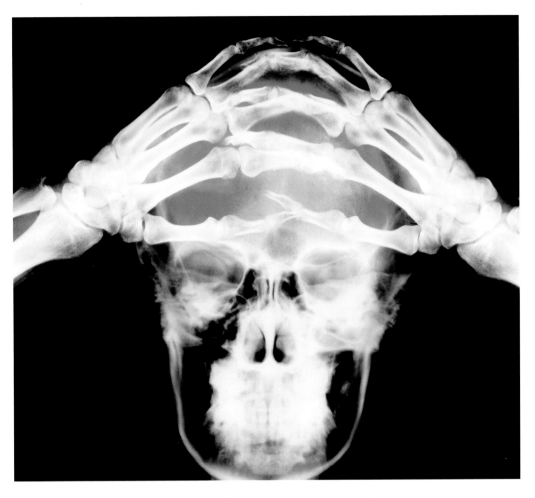

Tension-type headaches usually feel like an overall squeezing of the head.

Many people associate **stress** and strong emotions, such as fear or anger with headaches. But scientific studies have not proven these associations. More likely, people under extreme stress take less care to get the food, water, and rest they need. Their neglected bodies respond with a headache. However, people who suffer from a feeling of ongoing sadness called **depression** seem more likely to get headaches. That is probably due to the low levels of serotonin associated with depression.

Overtiredness is a major trigger of tension-type headaches as well as migraines. A quick nap can often help a mild headache go away.

Tension-type headaches may affect people in different ways. **Episodic** ones occur fewer than fifteen days a month. Usually, temporary conditions, such as being hungry, thirsty, or overtired during stressful periods, may bring on episodic headaches.

Chronic tension-type headaches occur fifteen or more days a month. They may be intense and affect both sides of the person's head. Medical experts believe untreated depression can cause chronic tension-type headaches. Those who suffer from them sometimes feel tired, dizzy, and **nauseated.** They often find it difficult to concentrate while a headache is going on.

Rebound headaches may occur when people overuse their headache medications to treat their chronic headaches.

Migraine Headaches

Migraine headaches are much less common than the tension type, but they are usually much more painful. According to the National Headache Foundation, approximately one in ten people suffers from migraine headaches. They account for half the doctor visits for headache treatment. In children, migraines are the cause of nearly all the doctor visits for headache pain. Three out of four migraine sufferers are women. Researchers believe that changing levels of chemicals called **hormones** are involved in the development of many migraine headaches in women. However, men get the majority of cluster headaches, which may be related to migraines. Drinking alcohol and smoking cigarettes can trigger cluster headaches.

Migraine headaches are almost always hereditary, which means the chance of having migraines can be passed on from parent to child. If both parents suffer from migraines, there is a 75 percent chance their children will, too. If only one parent gets migraines, the child has a 50 percent chance of getting migraines.

Migraine headaches often develop in a way that is different from other types of headaches. Some people who get migraines can often tell when one is coming before the pain actually

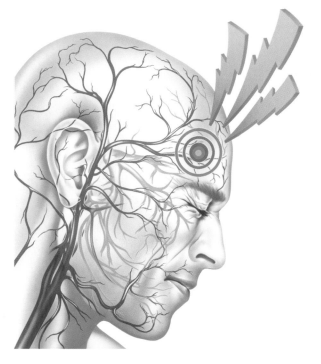

Nearly all migraines begin with concentrated pain on one spot of the head.

starts. During a pre-headache period called a **prodrome,** about 25 percent of adult migraine sufferers and 5 percent of children who get migraines may begin to experience an annoying ringing or buzzing sensation in the ears. They may also feel cold, tired, nauseated, and dizzy. During the prodrome, they often become very sensitive to light, noise, and odors right before the migraine begins. Some people get a tingling sensation in the arm and face. The skin of a person getting a migraine sometimes becomes flushed, or reddish in color, as the blood vessels in the head expand. This, in turn, stimulates the nerve endings in the head, which brings on the pain.

Although only 5 percent of children who get migraines have a visual experience known as an **aura,** about 25 percent of adult migraine sufferers get them. During an aura, a person may see flashing lights, zigzag lines, stars, patterns that go up and down, or areas of darkness. Some people describe their auras as "static" or "snow," similar to what you see on a television screen during bad reception. Aura symptoms usually last half an hour or so before the pain begins.

When the migraine does arrive, the pain is usually intense. Migraine headaches frequently begin as throbbing pain in the forehead or temples. The pain builds up gradually, sometimes moving to one side of the head, then spreading to the opposite side. During this period, the migraine sufferer may need

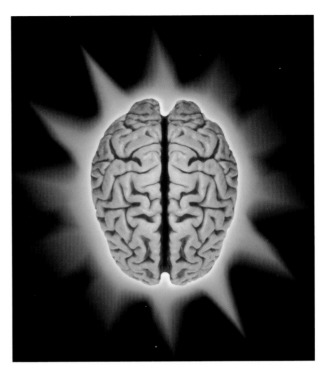

Thirty percent of migraine sufferers experience changing visual images.

to rest in a quiet room away from sources of noise and light, which intensify the pain. During the next few hours—one hour for children—the headache reaches its most painful level, then gradually becomes less severe. Migraines in adults may last for many hours or days or as long as a week. Although migraine pain is shorter and less intense for children than it is for adults, children are more likely than adults to experience mental confusion, nausea, chills, and sweating during a migraine attack.

Triggers are circumstances or factors that can set off a

The Cluster Headache

Cluster headaches, sometimes called "alarm-clock" headaches, often strike suddenly at the same time each day. Some actually awaken a person from sleep. These headaches arrive in clusters, or groups, of headaches that come and go, only to return again over a period of days or weeks. Cluster headache pain is intense and develops around one eye. The affected eye may water, become swollen and red, with its eyelid drooping. The pain often spreads to the entire side of the face.

The pain formed during a cluster headache is so severe that it may be difficult for the person with the headache to sit still. The headache usually lasts for about forty-five minutes, stops, then returns. Although cluster headaches are fairly rare, headache sufferers who get them may experience attacks over many years.

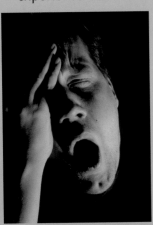

Men suffer the majority of cluster headaches, which usually last less than an hour but may return again and again.

migraine attack. The most common migraine triggers are hormonal changes in body chemistry, changing sleep and eating patterns, the environment, and personal habits, such as overuse of alcohol. Identifying, controlling, and possibly eliminating these triggers can help lessen the likelihood of a migraine attack.

SECONDARY HEADACHES

Ten percent of the headaches that people experience are symptoms of underlying medical conditions or disorders. Someone with a secondary headache may be suffering from an infectious illness, such as the flu, or pneumonia, which is a kind of lung infection. Several serious infections of the brain or nervous system can swell tissues in the head so much that a person gets a crushing headache, which many describe as the worst they have ever had.

Head injuries cause the brain to crash into the skull and damage blood vessels. Anyone who gets a headache or repeated headaches after a fall or other kind of accident should see a doctor right away. The person should also see a doctor if the headache does not go away quickly, if dizziness, blurred vision, or extreme tiredness follow, or if the headache goes away and then returns.

Head injuries suffered during sports or a bike, skateboard, or car accident require immediate medical attention.

In some cases, secondary headaches may be a sign of a brain abnormality such as a **brain tumor** or **aneurysm.**

Common Illnesses That Cause Headaches
Head colds, sinus infections in your nose, the flu, and other common illnesses, such as chicken pox, often arrive with a headache and other symptoms, including fever and muscle aches. The headache symptom reminds you that your body is

sick and needs attention. Usually bed rest, plenty of liquids, and headache pain medication help lessen the pain during common illnesses that bring headaches along with them.

Brain Infections That Cause Headaches

Several diseases that infect the brain can cause sudden and severe headaches. One of them, **bacterial meningitis,** is a swelling of the meninges that cover the brain and spinal cord. Bacteria or viruses cause meningitis, which can lead to brain damage. The symptoms of bacterial meningitis include a severe headache, as well as a stiff neck, fever, a possible rash, confusion, lack of energy, and eventual unconsciousness. Any intense headache accompanied by a very stiff neck requires urgent medical attention at a hospital. Bacterial meningitis can cause death within hours.

Other serious infections that invade parts of the brain and nervous system and cause severe headache symptoms include encephalitis, myelitis, and Rocky Mountain spotted fever.

Underlying Medical Conditions

When someone is suffering from certain ongoing medical conditions, one of the symptoms may be a headache. People with heart, lung, or kidney infections may get headaches when the infections cause inflammation that damages those organs. The headaches, along with other symptoms, signal that something is wrong. A person should see a doctor as soon as possible.

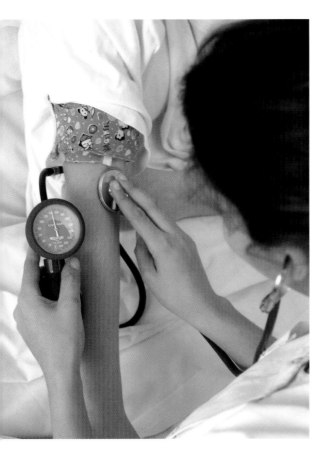

Headaches can be associated with high blood pressure, a condition in which blood flow to the body's organs—including the brain—is slowed down.

People who have arthritis and suffer from ongoing joint problems, especially near their necks, are prone to headaches. Headaches can also be a symptom associated with diabetes, a condition in which a person's body cannot handle the sugar level in the blood. Headaches may appear with other symptoms of diabetes, such as excessive hunger, thirst, tiredness, rapid weight loss, and frequent urination. All these symptoms, including the headaches, are signs that the body is in trouble.

Brain Abnormalities

Brain tumors are rare abnormal growths inside the brain. A brain tumor may be made up of cells that are cancerous and growing wildly. Even if a tumor is not cancerous, any tumor can damage the brain and cause pressure and pain in the surrounding areas. Since the brain does not experience pain,

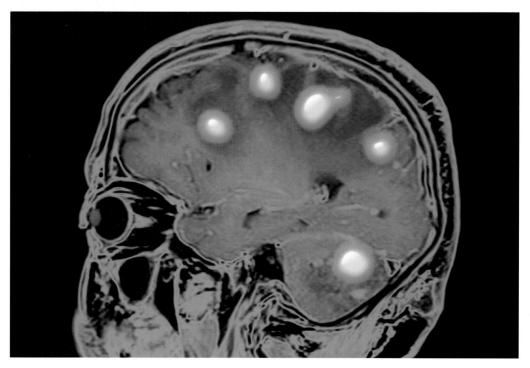

The multiple brain tumors in this magnetic resonance image (MRI) cause swelling, which may bring on sudden, severe headaches.

brain tumors may grow unnoticed. However, as the brain tumor grows, it takes up space and presses on nerves surrounding the brain. That can lead to a severe headache, which may be sudden or which may become worse over time. Anyone with these headache symptoms should visit a doctor as soon as possible.

A brain aneurysm is a balloon-like bulge or weakness that appears in the wall of a blood vessel in the brain. A brain aneurysm can cause extreme, sudden head pain called a "thunderclap" headache right before the aneurysm bursts and begins to **hemorrhage,** or bleed severely, into the brain. If not treated immediately, a burst aneurysm often leads to unconsciousness or death. This condition can also cause a serious medical event called a **stroke.** A stroke damages brain cells that may control movement, memory, and speech. Strokes disable and kill many victims each year.

Fortunately, most headaches are not cause for alarm. But whether primary or secondary, any headache is a pain! Most people can live with occasional headaches that do not require any treatment. For other individuals, headaches come frequently or arrive with intense pain. These headache sufferers may want to learn about ways to prevent or treat them.

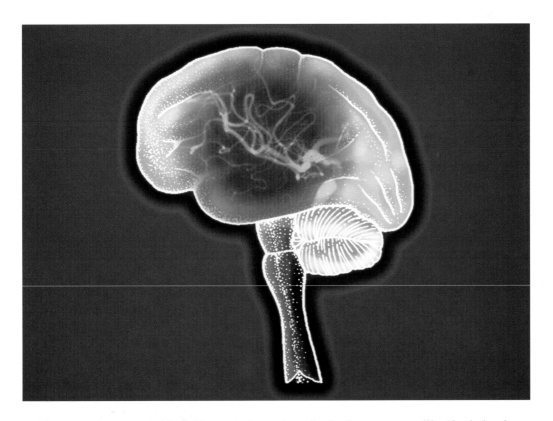

Sudden, ongoing, severe headaches may be a sign of a brain aneurysm, like the bulge in the blood vessel shown in this computer image of a brain.

Some Common Headaches

Here are a few kinds of primary headaches that many people experience once in a while. Some preventive measures may keep them from developing. If they do develop, certain treatments can lessen or shorten the duration of the headache pain.

Type	Triggers
Physical tension headache	Sitting or holding one position too long
Physical activity headache	Overexercising; not drinking enough water or eating enough food on days of heavy physical exercise
Eyestrain headache	Staring too long at the television or computer screen or a book
Sore-jaw headache	Grinding teeth during the day or during sleep due to worry; crooked teeth that affect biting
Rebound headaches	Stopping certain medications; stopping beverages containing a chemical called **caffeine**
Ice-cream headaches	Eating ice cream or gulping down icy drinks too fast.

Treatment	Prevention
Move around; stretch; ask a parent for a small dose of an over-the-counter headache medication if the headache does not go away on its own.	Plan fifteen-minute breaks before sitting down to study, watching television, working at a computer, or carrying a heavy backpack. Slowly, gently roll around head and shoulders
Eat lightly before exercising; take frequent breaks during heavy exercise; drink plenty of water before, during, and after exercising.	Build up exercise gradually; know your limits.
Move back from the television or computer monitor; look away every ten minutes; get your eyes checked; ask a parent for a small dose of an over-the-counter headache medication if the headache does not go away on its own.	Alternate sitting activities with walking, running, and moving around. See an eye doctor.
Do relaxation exercises for the jaw and head; use a special device—from the dentist—to stop the grinding or biting.	Deal with feelings by talking about them. See a dentist.
Slowly reduce (if approved by a doctor) medications and beverages containing caffeine.	Drink water and juices instead of sodas, teas, and chocolate drinks and coffee with caffeine. Under parental supervision, take the lowest effective doses of medications, such as painkillers.
No treatment—they just go away quickly.	Lick ice cream and sip icy drinks slowly.

3

THE HISTORY OF HEADACHES

Humans have been suffering from headaches and seeking treatment for them for thousands of years. One archeological finding shows that as early as 7000 BCE, doctors in Egypt treated headache patients by drilling a hole into the patient's skull to release the pain! Historians suggest that this procedure may have been performed to let out evil spirits from the head—some ancient people believed that the evil spirits caused the pain.

Other findings show that the Egyptians sometimes pressed fried fish or warm goat droppings to the painful area. One treatment involved using a strip of linen to fasten a clay crocodile holding grain in its mouth around the patient's head. The strip of linen contained the names of the gods who were supposed to cure sickness and disease. While there is no evidence suggesting that either of these approaches worked, there is a possibility the clay crocodile treatment might have relieved some of the pain through pressure on the scalp.

The Greek physician Hippocrates, was the first to write down the visual symptoms of a migraine headache. He described an aura—or shining light—that usually occurred in the right eye. He also described the throbbing sensation around the temples and forehead that is familiar to migraine sufferers today.

Hippocrates, who stated that all illnesses stemmed from natural imbalances in the body, also believed headaches could be traced to fluids or vapors that originated in the liver and spread to the head. He called these fluids or vapors "humors." To treat headaches, he recommended draining blood from the patient through bloodletting. It was believed

HIPOCRATI COO

The Greek physician Hippocrates identified some of symptoms of migraine headaches before there was a medical name for them.

that this would relieve the pressure of fluids in the body and the headache would go away. An alternative way to ease pressure in the body was to apply blood-sucking leeches to the patient's skin. The leeches sucked blood from the patient's body, again to remove fluids that pressed on the head.

During the Middle Ages (beginning around the late 1000s CE and lasting until the late 1400s CE), doctors used a combination of vinegar and a drug called opium to treat

Massage, air, and rest have been among the recommended headache remedies throughout the ages.

patients with headaches. First, they wet the patient's forehead with vinegar to open the skin pores. Then they applied a soft, moist, heated cloth soaked in opium to the patient's head.

After the mid-1600s, some doctors discovered that blood circulated throughout the human body through a network of blood vessels. In 1672, an English physician named Thomas Willis suggested that a number of factors could trigger the onset of migraines. These ranged from changes in the seasons and atmospheric conditions to diet and heredity. He understood that parents could pass on various conditions to their children.

Willis was the first doctor to suggest that the swelling of blood vessels in the head caused what we now know as migraine headaches. Willis's idea about **dilated** blood vessels became known as the **vascular,** or "vessel" theory of headaches.

Many doctors since Willis's time accepted his vascular theory in one form or another. However, most experts now believe that dilated or narrow blood vessels associated with headaches are a *result* of nerve activity in the brain, not their cause.

Many experts have recently taken another look back at the findings of a doctor who published a paper on headaches in 1873. That study presented a more accurate theory about headaches than Willis did. In his paper, Edward Living linked migraine headaches with other neurological disorders, such as dizziness, sleeplessness, epilepsy, lightheadedness, and fainting. Experts are finding more evidence that problems in the nervous system that lead to headaches begin in the **cerebral cortex** of the brain. Previously, many thought that problems were in the blood vessels.

An Unusual Headache Treatment

Many scientists accepted Thomas Willis's theory that the swelling of blood vessels caused headaches—particularly migraines. But actual treatments varied. Erasmus Darwin, grandfather of the famous scientist Charles Darwin, came up with one unique treatment. In the late 1770s, he proposed that doctors spin migraine sufferers around in a compartment. This supposedly relieved pressure in the head by forcing blood down to the feet. This was much like the "salt and pepper shaker" rides you might have experienced at an amusement park. Historians are not sure whether or not this unusual treatment worked.

IMPROVEMENT IN HEADACHE TREATMENTS

Until the mid-1800s, most scientists and physicians focused on the causes of migraine headaches and the possible ways to treat them. They paid less attention to what was called the "common headache," known today as the "tension-type headache."

In the late 1800s, neurologists in England began to examine common headaches more closely. Many believed ordinary headaches stemmed directly from too much thinking, excessive emotions, or worry about being sick. Although these ideas may seem a little far-fetched, many of them are being debated today. It may be true that difficult personal problems, as well as psychological causes—rather than strictly physical ones—cause headaches.

Treatments the neurologists recommended ranged from strict bed rest and vigorous physical activity to cold baths. Among the medications they prescribed for treatment were opium and marijuana, which are

Le Mal de Tête.

The English cartoonist, Cruickshank, drew this picture in 1819 of a headache sufferer being attacked by demons.

considered dangerous substances today and are also illegal.

In the late 1880s, William Gowers, a British physician, came up with a treatment that became known as the "Gowers mixture." It was basically a solution of nitroglycerin—a thick, pale yellow, explosive liquid used in dynamite—and alcohol, mixed with other chemical ingredients. Some patients found it effective.

At the beginning of the twentieth century, a prominent Canadian physician named Sir William Osler believed abnormalities in the scalp and neck muscles caused common headaches. In the 1940s, an American physician named Harold Wolff grew convinced that Osler was right. He conducted experiments demonstrating that uncontrollable tightening of muscles in the scalp and neck caused headaches. He called these types of headaches muscle-contraction headaches.

For the next forty years,

WOLCOTT'S INSTANT PAIN ANNIHILATOR.

Headache remedies were around long before ibuprofen and other modern headache remedies came into use.

Doctors were convinced that muscle tightness caused most headaches until machines like the electromyograph showed that many headache sufferers had no muscle tension.

most doctors accepted Wolff's explanation. However, thanks to advances in medical diagnostic equipment, new studies challenged some of Wolff's ideas. These studies suggested that some common headache sufferers showed little or no muscle tension.

Since the 1980s, some medical researchers have argued that there is no basic difference in the causes of common tension-type headaches and most migraine headaches. The debate continues. However, in the past twenty-five years, the diagnosis and treatment of every variety of headache have advanced more than in all the previous centuries combined. A better understanding of headaches and their causes has led to a variety of tried-and-true treatments, ranging from more effective medication to helpful exercises and healthier diets. Some drugs today specifically regulate hormones, help keep blood vessels from becoming inflamed, or help maintain levels of helpful neurotransmitters that ease pain. These are a long way from treatments such as applying fried fish or warm goat droppings or drilling a hole in a headache sufferer's head!

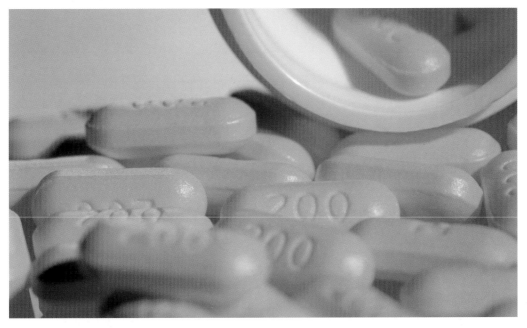

In the past, doctors had to prescribe ibuprofen for their headache patients. Now lower doses of ibuprofen are available over the counter without a doctor's prescription.

4

LIVING WITH HEADACHES

ven a mild tension-type headache can make it hard to concentrate, work, enjoy yourself, talk with friends, or enjoy a meal. People who suffer from regular, chronic headaches or from migraines may miss school, work, and social gatherings. They often find it difficult to take pleasure in everyday activities while they are suffering from a headache.

Some types of headaches may interfere with everyday life. Many treatments available today can help.

Most people who get occasional mild headaches do not usually need to seek medical help unless they are sick with another condition that needs treatment. However, for those who cannot live normally because of migraines or frequent tension-type headaches, preventive steps and medical treatment can sometimes keep the pain from starting or relieve pain if it does begin. New research and technologies are helping doctors learn more about the causes of headaches and the best treatments for them.

Some doctors ask headache sufferers to keep track of their headaches for a month or so before treatment begins. The patients write down the date and time that each headache occurred, along with the length of time the headache lasted. They answer certain questions. Did the headache return? Was the pain dull, constant, or stabbing? When did they last eat and drink before the headache arrived? Did they start or stop any medications before the headache began? What sleep patterns did they experience? Did they engage in any particular physical activity before the pain started? Also, was any medication taken to relieve the pain? What was it, and did it work? The answers to these questions, in the form of a diary, can be a valuable tool in helping a doctor to make a diagnosis and recommend effective treatment.

During a patient's visit to the doctor's or to a headache clinic, the doctor may review his or her notes or ask questions about the headaches before performing a physical exam. The doctor will check the patient's ear, eyes, nose, and throat for possible infections. The doctor may perform a motor exam and

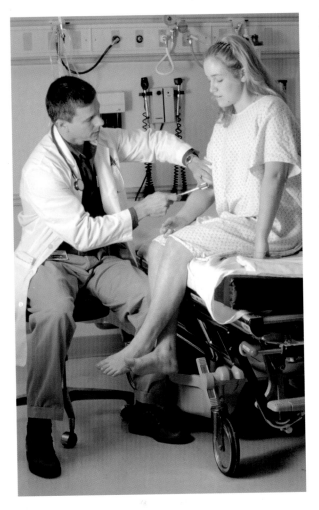

Anyone who sees a doctor for problem headaches will usually undergo a physical examination and an interview to determine the cause and patterns of headaches.

ask the patient to move specific muscles or to walk around the room. This checks for possible problems with the brain or nervous system. The doctor may also ask the patient to wiggle his or her toes. Other tests the doctor may request are X rays, blood tests, and head scans.

A computerized axial tomography scan, or **CAT scan,** is a special kind of X ray that takes three-dimensional pictures of body parts, such as the brain. During a CAT scan of the brain, the patient lies flat on a platform while a machine goes around his or her head, taking pictures. By looking at the results of a CAT scan, a doctor can tell immediately if there are any signs of a brain tumor, bleeding in the brain, or stroke.

Magnetic resonance imaging, or **MRI,** is a technique that

A doctor may order and review MRI brain scans to rule out tumors or aneurysms as the cause of a patient's headaches.

takes pictures of structures inside the body. Besides detecting possible brain bleeding, a tumor, or a stroke, an MRI can also identify areas that suffer from decreased blood flow levels. This is important in helping migraine sufferers, who experience reduced flow of blood to the brain.

After an examination, the doctor might also recommend that the patient see a neurologist. This specialist will examine the brain, the spinal cord, nerves, and the muscles related to the nerves.

Warning Signs of Serious Headaches

Call the doctor if a headache

- awakens you from sleep and lasts for hours.

- accompanies an extremely painful, stiff neck.

- starts with a head injury but continues after the injury heals.

- occurs with dizziness, confusion, or unusual sleepiness.

- feels like the worst one you ever had.

- appears with severe vomiting.

- keeps worsening or goes away, then returns several times in a week.

HEADACHE PREVENTION

You may never need to see a doctor about regular headaches if you can prevent them in the first place. Some of the best ways to try preventing headaches are the easiest. First, make sure you get the sleep you need. How do you know how much you need? You should be able to get up in the morning without too much difficulty. You should be able to stay awake at school and not need daily naps when you get home. If you always feel tired and get headaches, too, try going to bed half an hour earlier each night. See if the headaches stop. Develop regular sleeping habits—go to bed and get up at the same time, including on weekends.

Eat healthy foods at regular mealtimes and snack times, though this is not always easy

Headaches and sleep habits are closely connected. Falling asleep during the day can be a sign that a person needs more sleep at night.

with different school lunch schedules. Start each day with something healthy to eat for breakfast, such as whole-grain cereal, whole-wheat toast, fruit, or an egg. A healthy snack such as cut-up fruit midmorning or midafternoon can keep you going if you have a late lunchtime or dinnertime. It is very important to drink plenty of water throughout the day and drink additional fluids if it is hot out or if you are physically active.

Get up and move around every fifteen minutes or so when you watch television, use the computer, or study for a long

Regular, healthy eating habits can prevent many headaches.

time. Since eyestrain is sometimes associated with headaches, get your eyes checked if they constantly feel tired. Give your eyes a rest when you are studying or working at the computer.

Although the connection between stress and headaches is still being studied, take good care of your body all the time by developing healthy habits. Learn how to relax by playing, taking deep breaths, just sitting, or doing some physical activity that you enjoy, such as walking or running. These activities can lessen stress and worry. Physical activities are known to increase the number of pain-relieving chemicals circulating through the body.

Tell an adult in your family or at school if you constantly feel sad or upset about something. Depression and headaches often appear together.

Triggers

It is difficult for doctors and scientists to say exactly what causes a headache, but they do know that certain triggers can lead to one. A trigger is something that someone is sensitive to, and it differs from person to person. Among the common triggers that often lead to headaches are irregular sleep patterns, insufficient sleep, or skipped meals. Oversensitivity to odors and specific sights and sounds may be triggers for migraine sufferers.

For some time, many headache sufferers and their doctors believed that certain foods set off migraine attacks, especially prepared foods that contained certain chemicals. There is increasing evidence now that dehydration and disrupted eating patterns, such as skipped meals, are more likely to irritate nerves, setting off a

Eating healthy, drinking plenty of water, and getting some exercise with friends are great headache preventers.

Some odors, such as cigarette smoke, are associated with both allergies and with headaches.

chain of migraine symptoms. Most neurologists and doctors at headache centers now advise migraine sufferers, especially children, to develop healthy, regular sleep and eating habits.

Many doctors, as well as their migraine patients, believe that smells and odors triggered migraines. Some headache sufferers avoid gasoline fumes, car exhaust, perfume, hairspray, flowers, cigarette smoke, and certain food smells like that of deep-fried fish. However, new research shows that **hypersensitivity** to these odors is the problem. Studies have not proved that these odors cause the headaches. It is likely that the person was developing a headache anyway.

Many headache sufferers associate emotional stress with the onset of headaches. Current medical research indicates that this may be due more to loss of sleep and disrupted eating patterns that people experience during times of stress. However, anyone who is suffering from ongoing depression, rather than everyday worries, should seek treatment. Depression and a tendency to get migraines are connected, probably due to abnormalities in serotonin levels.

In the past, doctors and their patients believed changes in weather patterns might also trigger a headache. There is no reliable scientific evidence for this.

TREATMENT THROUGH MEDICATION

As any headache sufferer will tell you, avoiding situations that can cause a headache is not that easy. By the time a person realizes he or she is sick or too tired, hungry, or thirsty, it is often too late. The pain has already started. Thanks to advances in medicine since the 1980s, there are a variety of drugs that do a tremendous job offering pain relief.

Doctors recommend trying what are known as first-line medications. These may be over-the-counter pain relievers, called OTCs, or medication issued on a doctor's written order, called a prescription. Supermarkets and drugstores sell over-the-counter headache painkillers. However, patients can only get a prescription drug from a registered pharmacist who

A pharmacist can help a headache sufferer sort out the many different headache remedies available over the counter.

also provides instructions for taking the medication.

Medications that offer relief from headache pain that has already started are called **abortive medications.** They are available as both OTC pain relievers and prescription drugs. They usually come in tablet or capsule form. For abortive medications to be effective, it is important that they be taken at the first sign of a headache. Once the user swallows the capsules or tablets, it takes about twenty to sixty minutes to feel relief. That is because it takes that long for the medication to first pass through the digestive system before entering the bloodstream. The blood then carries the medication to the sources of pain.

One of the most effective over-the-counter medications is ibuprofen. It is an **anti-inflammatory** drug that slows the swelling of blood vessels in the head. For that reason, it can be very effective in treating migraines and other headache types, depending on the dosage. A doctor can advise migraine sufferers of the right dose for their ages and their types of migraine. Children should not take aspirin for a headache. It is not as effective as ibuprofen and is associated with a serious medical condition called Reye's syndrome.

If first-line, lower-strength abortive medications do not work, doctors will recommend second-line medications. Some of these medications contain **ergotamine.** This ingredient keeps the blood vessels in the head from swelling and pressing on the nerve endings near the brain and scalp.

A special fungus is applied to plants such as rye to produce ergotamine, a chemical used .in some migraine medications.

Doctors have discovered that **anti-epileptic** medication can sometimes help migraine sufferers. People who have a neurological condition called **epilepsy** take these medications to control **seizures,** which occur when abnormal electrical activity in the brain causes sudden muscle tightening.

Some adult headache sufferers take daily **antidepressants** to regulate depression. Doctors prescribe one type, a **tricyclic,** to help prevent some migraine headaches. However, questions have been raised about the widespread use of antidepressants for children and adolescents. So any antidepressant treatment must be given under strict medical supervision. Helping children who suffer from migraines to develop regular sleeping and eating habits is a better preventive approach than prescribed medications.

While taking abortive medications can certainly provide relief from headache pain, there are risks in taking too many of them. Some people overuse headache medications and need higher and higher doses to control their headache pain. They become dependent on these higher doses. Kidney and liver failure and other serious medical problems have been linked to overuse of both over-the-counter and prescribed headache medications. For chronic headache sufferers who experience at least fifteen headaches a month, doctors recommend preventive drugs that keep headache pain from starting.

HEADACHE CLINICS

Some sufferers of chronic headaches, migraines, or cluster headaches decide to seek treatment at a headache clinic. There, a team of doctors, nurses, and possibly psychologists or social workers—who specialize in treating emotional problems—meet with the patient. The doctor will interview the patient, record his or her medical history, and order tests to determine the physical causes of the headaches. Others on the team may offer counseling and support to patients whose headaches are associated with depression or who are addicted to headache pain medication and get rebound headaches.

A visit to a headache clinic or specialist may be advisable for people whose headaches interfere with their daily lives.

For depressed patients, the team may draw up a plan to treat the condition with antidepressants that can also help with headaches. If the patient is suffering from rebound headaches due to dependency on headache painkillers, the team will help the patient slowly withdraw from these medications. The professionals at a headache clinic will also recommend lifestyle changes in sleep and eating habits to help prevent the headaches. The doctor may also prescribe effective medications for those who suffer from severe, repeated migraines that require stronger medications.

ALTERNATIVE THERAPIES AND SELF-HELP

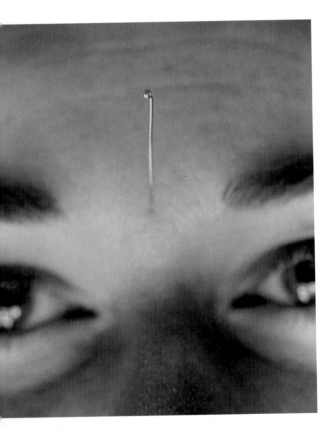

The needles used in acupuncture to treat many pains, including headache pain, are so thin, patients barely feel pain them.

Doctors may or may not recommend nonmedical alternative therapies for treating headaches. Some headache sufferers believe they are effective in providing headache pain relief. Seeing what works can be a trial-and-error process. One effective headache treatment you can give yourself is the simplest. If your headache strikes when you are at home, or there is a bed in the nurse's office at school, just lie down for a while, with a cold cloth on your head, and take a short nap. Often you will find the headache is gone when you wake up. Many headache sufferers have found massage therapy provides relief for headaches, though studies continue to explore the effectiveness of this treatment.

For centuries, Chinese practitioners have used a treatment called **acupuncture** to treat many medical conditions. Acupuncture is now widely available in the United States. The practitioner, called an acupuncturist, inserts extremely thin needles—which are painless—at various points in the body to disrupt pain signals. With occasional acupuncture treatments, some headache sufferers say they find relief from chronic headaches and migraines, though scientific studies have not yet proved the effectiveness of acupuncture. Acupuncture should only be performed by a trained professional.

Biofeedback is another alternative therapy that has been helpful for some headache sufferers. It is a painless procedure in which machines and computers operated by a trained therapist monitor exactly what is going on inside a patient's body.

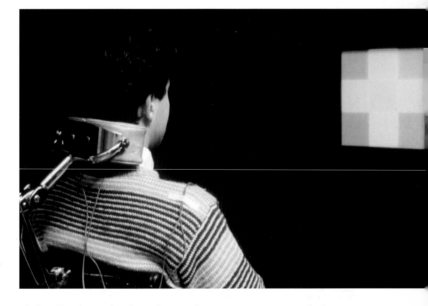

Biofeedback, and other alternative treatments, may help headache sufferers pay attention to their bodies' needs.

An ice pack may soothe the pain of swollen blood vessels associated with headaches.

Headache sufferers can learn about their brain waves and observe which relaxation exercises work best in relieving stress. They can then try those whenever they begin to get headaches. In addition, patients visualize what happens to them when a migraine strikes.

All of these treatments may seem effective because of something called the **placebo effect.** This happens in treatments for many conditions, as well as for headaches. When people believe that certain treatments are helpful, they may experience temporary relief of their symptoms.

While there is no cure for headaches, that does not mean that a headache sufferer cannot live a normal, active, fun-filled, productive life. With a combination of proven prevention and treatment methods, relief is definitely in sight.

GLOSSARY

abortive medications—The medications that offer relief from headache pain that has already started.

acupuncture—The use of thin needles to puncture the body in order to relieve pain.

aneurysm—A balloon-like bulge or weakness that appears in a blood vessel wall, frequently in the brain.

antidepressants—The preventive medications that can be effective in treating chronic tension headaches and migraines, as well as depression.

anti-epileptic—The type of medication used to treat a neurological disorder called epilepsy.

anti-inflammatory—The ability to reduce swelling.

aura—A visual warning that a migraine is about to occur.

bacterial meningitis—A disease that develops when bacteria infect the brain and spinal cord covering called the meninges.

biofeedback—A technological procedure that gives pain information back to the patient so that he or she can adjust responses to pain.

blood vessels—The tubes that carry blood to organs and tissues throughout the body.

brain tumor—An abnormal growth in the brain that may press against blood vessel walls.

caffeine—A chemical found in plants, such as tea and coffee plants, that stimulates the nervous system.

CAT scan—A special kind of X ray that takes pictures of the brain. CAT stands for computerized axial tomography.

cerebral cortex—The outer layer of the brain.

chronic—The description of a medical condition that lasts a long time or reappears.

cluster headaches—The kinds of migraine which arrive in groups and are very painful.

dehydrated—The condition in which the body lacks the water it needs to function properly.

depression—A medical condition with symptoms that include a long-lasting feeling of sadness, hopelessness,and tiredness.

dilated—Expanded or widened.

dopamine—A chemical messenger in the body that helps control blood flow.

electromyograph (EMG)—The electronic medical device that shows the electrical activity of muscles.

endorphins—The chemicals that allow the brain's automatic pain control system to work.

epilepsy—A neurological disorder that may set off seizures, which are sudden, unplanned tightening of muscles.

episodic—Happening at irregular times.

ergotamine—A drug made from a fungus that helps prevent blood vessels in the head from pressing against the nerves.

fungus—A kind of organism that feeds on organic matter.

hemorrhage—To bleed severely.

hormones—A type of chemical involved in bodily functions.

hypersensitivity—A tendency to be physically responsive to particular outside stimulation.

ibuprofen—A kind of man-made painkiller.

meninges—The protective covering of the brain and spinal cord.

migraine—A worsening headache with throbbing pain that usually begins in one area of the forehead then spreads to the opposite side.

MRI—An X ray that takes pictures of every part of the body. MRI stands for magnetic resonance imaging.

nauseated—A feeling of stomach upset with an urge to vomit.

nerve cells—The cells that make up a nerve and help it to send messages between the spinal cord and brain and other parts of the body.

nervous system—The body system that includes the brain, spinal cord, and nerves.

neurologist—A doctor who specializes in disorders associated with the nervous system, particularly disorders in the brain.

neurotransmitters—The chemicals that carry messages among nerve cells throughout the body and the brain and spinal cord.

placebo effect—A positive effect due to a patient's belief in the treatment.

prescription—The doctor's written order for medication.

primary headaches—The headaches that are not due to underlying causes.

prodrome—The warning sign that a migraine is about to occur.

rebound headaches—The types of headaches that return after medication wears off. These headaches are caused by a dependence on the medication.

secondary headaches—The headaches that are due to underlying causes such as illnesses, infections, or existing medical conditions.

seizures—A sudden tightening of muscles that may result in unconsciousness.

serotonin—The neurotransmitter that helps keep blood vessels narrow.

stress—A feeling of emotional pressure and tension.

stroke—The interruption of blood flow to the brain.

symptoms—Any changes in the body that signal the presence of an illness.

tension-type headaches—The most common forms of headache, which are likely caused by chemical and nerve activity in the brain.

tricyclic—A particular class of antidepressant drugs.

trigeminal nerve system—The human body's major pain pathway.

trigger—Setting off pain due to certain situations or conditions.

vascular—Describing the system of blood vessels within the human body.

FIND OUT MORE

ORGANIZATIONS

American Council for Headache Education (ACHE)
19 Mantua Road
Mount Royal, NJ 08061
(800) 255-ACHE
(856) 423-0258
www.achenet.org

National Headache Foundation (NHF)
820 North Orleans, Suite 217
Chicago, IL 60610
(888) NHF-5552
www.headaches.org

National Institute of Neurological Disorders and Stroke
P.O. Box 5801
Bethesda, MD 20824
(800) 352-9424
www.ninds.nih.gov

BOOKS

Diamond, Seymour, M.D. and Amy Diamond, *Headaches and Your Child: The Complete Guide to Understanding and Treating Migraines and Other Headaches in Children and Adolescents*. New York: Fireside Books, Simon and Schuster, 2001.

Guidetti, Vincenzo. *Headache and Migraine in Childhood and Adolescence*. London, England: Martin Dunitz Limited, The Livery House, 2002.

Moe, Barbara. *Everything You Need to Know about Migraines and Other Headaches*. New York: The Rosen Publishing Group, 2000.

Sheen, Barbara. *Headaches*. Farmington Hills, Michigan: Lucent Books, Thomas Gale, 2004.

Votava, Andrea. *Coping with Migraines and Other Headaches*. New York: The Rosen Publishing Group, 2000.

Winner, Paul and David Rothner, M.D., *Headache in Children and Adolescents*. Ontario, Canada: B. C. Decker, 2000.

Web Sites

Kids Get Headaches, Too! (American Council for Headache Education)
http://achenet.org/kids

Migraine Awareness Group: A National Understanding for Migraineurs (MAGNUM)
http://www.migraines.org

Oooh, Your Aching Head (KidsHealth)
http://www.kidshealth.org/kid/ill_injure/sick/headache.html

INDEX

Page numbers for illustrations are in **boldface**

ABOUT THE AUTHOR

Rick Petreycik has written several books for Marshall Cavendish Benchmark. He has also written articles on history, music, film, travel, and business for *American Legacy*, *Rolling Stone*, *Yankee*, *Disney Magazine*, *The Oxford American*, and *The Hartford Courant*. He lives in Connecticut with his wife and daughter, who suffers from occasional migraines.